Flyaringaron

By
Wilnona Marie

Willette's Stories
P.O Box 5712
Annapolis, Maryland 21403

Willette's Stories

Printed in the United States

First book printing: *April 2005*

This Book is Dedicated to:

This book is dedicated to all those who believed in my dreams for the last fifteen years. To my family (Roshae, Ann, & Jamie) To my loving husband Christopher, my in laws and my editor Linda Leonard who made my words more than black letters on a page, but gave them a life of their own.   I must mention the ladies at the book club because they didn't think I would.

Chapter 1

"Yal come back here with that ball."

"Catch us if you can."   Jermey taunted his uncle.
"You know if I catch you, I'm going to tickle you to death."
Chirstian exaggerated the end of his statement, and the boys
chuckled as Jermey sent the pigskin sailing through the air.
Christian faked loosing his footing and fell into the fried golden
strands of grass.   Jeremey's brother Neilosn's fingers closed
around the laces. With his head up, not missing a beat he took
off toward the end zone, dashing between the defense, leaving
the imaginary team to choke on his dust.

"Touch down!" he shouted throwing the ball to the ground,
and doing a little dance. "No one can catch iron head."

Christian dusted off his slacks, he slipped into the house to
see his ex-sister in law,   and change his jeans.   Julia was
mixing up a cake from the box, she was caught of guard when
he entered the kitchen and wrap his arms around her in a play
brother sister manner.

"Wuz up, sis?"

"You scared me." Jocularly she smacked him leaving behind a
red mark.

"That slapped scared me."   He stuck his finger in the soupy batter, licked his finger, with his mouth full of the yellowish mixture   he continued speaking " It hurt."

She grabbed the spatula behind him on the counter   he was leaned against,   and began scraping the sides of the bowl into a nine inch round pan. "That was from Karen. You never called."

"I haven't called in three years, what made her think that was going to change."

"You picked up the kid last week and took her to the zoo, and dropped her off with not so much as a hello."

"Her fiancée was sitting on the couch, and if her memory serves her right   he said if I talked to her he would kill me."   He reached for the bowl to finish of f the lines of quickly drying remains that the spatula left behind.

"He didn't mean it."

"I'm not going to test it."

     She gently placed the pan on the top oven rack, and checked the temperature, then closed the door on the golden cake soup.

"She loves you!"

"So she says, but I think that she needs a babysitter for her kid."

     Christian non verbally volunteered to wash the dishes. She

sat at the broke down   second hand table.
"How's . . ."
"Derrek? Fine."
"Is he . . .?"

"Still with her? No! He has moved on   to some eighteen year old, great body, no brain, but not half as wonderful to him as you."

HE could her sigh.   He had told a little lie, but for Julia it was worth it she deserved a laugh at his expense, that didn't involve visitation rights.   It was harmless.   Julia still loved Derrek and she had a right to.   They had been married for eight years and nine months, he had cheated since the "I Do" , it was only fair that she get some payback.   Truthfuly Derrek had taken off two weeks from work and was now on a Caribbean beach.

"So where are you taking Jeremy and Neilson?"

"To the airfield for that field trip I promised them."

"Thank you.   Jermey really wanted to go with his class, but I really couldn't afford it then."

"I told you I would give you a hand."

"Thanks Christian."   He placed the dish on the bath towel spread across the pressed wood countertops. "The envelope on the table belongs to you. Get a pedicure or something for you.   The kids will stay with me tonight."

"If you weren't so young.   .."

"I'd be Derrek."

"Maybe."

Christian shuffled down the   linoleum hallway that was to small for two people to pass, and tumbled into the matchbox bathroom.   Her house resembled a dirty doll house with those plastic collectible accessories. Except the collector never did get around to finishing what should have been adorable. He tossed his old sweats in the dirty hamper and   pulled the jeans on.

Julia called the children to the door, so they could get washed up to go.   Her extra waitress   shift started in   forty five minutes.   They had to be gone in twenty.   Reluctantly Julia joined her boys in a quick game of catch. Excluding the possibilities of this evening this was   definitely a highlight. Neilson practiced his form for passing.   Julia congratulated him for the decent throw as she   confiscated the ball to divert attention to the bathroom sink.   Once they were in the restroom uncle Christian would take over.

At whirlwind speed to Julia the boys were dressed in their dad's latest gift shirts, khakis, and their hair combed to look like a carbon copy of their interim guardian. They stood beside the screen door. Julia looked them over.

"Mommy," Neilson spoke excitedly. "Christian is letting us spend the night in his new house."

"Yes I know." She bent down to her youngest level. "Now give me a kiss."

He pressed his lips to her cheek. "And you Mr. Man."   Jeremy smooched her on the left cheek.

Christian rattled the keys reminding them to hurry along their goodbyes.   She stood erect and demanded

" You take care of my boys."]

"I will."   Christian followed the pattern and kissed her in the fore head. "I promise them tomorrow at seven as clean and sweet as I took them today."

He opened the screen door and the boys filed one behind the other, swiftly shut the door after them.

" Promise me You'll be careful."
  "I don't think there is much trobule you can get into as a waitress.   The sausages aren't going to attack me."

He winked at her, and   laughed quietly.

"Say hey! To karen for me."

As he walked out the door she practicly whispered "I'll be safe. I won't take any uncalculated risk like last week. I have to come home to my boys."

"Thank you." He walked down her front steps looking back and waving, they piled into the car, and took off down the street. She could still see them when the passenger's window shattered. Her thoughts consisted of   of her children only were they hurt. Were they conscious, how much was the hospital bill going cost   they didn't have insurance.?

    Her stiletto's clickty clacked against the cement sidewalks and way back in the corner of her mind there was a barely audible line of words that hummed in her head. *Maybe It's dad? He wouldn't play such a trick?*

Chapter 2

Mist from the indoor waterfall of sparkling diamond droplets poured out tipped over the edge of rocks spritzing the high counsel with it's refreshment.   Though at this moment there was no quenching the thirst of the land.

"Sir, your father's health worsens, and request that you direct our armies in the next battle."   Gilbur had told the young man   in the aging general's tent   a week ago.   Now he stood before those three hundred times his age to tell them to unify under him and accept the ruler ship the current powers that be.

"Fellow gentlemen we have had our difficulties in the past. . . "

A boulder smashed against the side of the fortifications they had assembled in.   Gilbur gestured for the novice speaker to continue.

"But we all have problems.   That is a unifying factor right there."   He waited for the laughter his predecessor would have gotten. Respectfully they allowed his highness to speak. "In turmoil therein lies desperation, chaos, blame, genocides, and irrational violence.   When desperation runs amuck. Brothers we well know that these times plague us now. As a united band weaved together we can stand   and give our citizens a means for hope my ill father would like the kingdom to have for one day." A slow clap started similar to the one often seen in one our world's movie pictures. The prince beamed. He had done it. He was going to save his world the way his father had told him, in word. Beautifully articulated words. Be it for a day, an hour or a minute his father would . . . Once again the building shook and a stench so commonly smelled these days of war filled the room. Panic ensued. Next would be the gas. Citizens nobles of peace, and kingship favor would fall. Die. The prince wanted to fall first, he wanted to succumb to the non-lethal aroma, instead of reporting to the mostly vacant castle.

Two "favorables" attired in long crushed velvet robes tied with a gold sash took flight from either side of the podium scooping up the crowned heir and forcibly pushing him toward the   solid stone wall.
"What are you doing; I want to die!"
"We can't let you . They will have won if you perish."
"Well you're aren't doing much better . This is a brick wall.."

"It's Dana stone. Sir. Walk."

He did as he was told.   Behind him subjects scurried every which direction.   Hoping to escape to their sprawling estates. Body guards fought amongst each other   to   move their charges thru the mob and to secret tunnels assigned to each family head present.   A few sons took up arms and slayed their father for their own life sake.

The prince walked toward the wall his guards standing shoulder to shoulder behind him.   The dana stone sucked half their body in and started replicating them dna cell by cell.   In a minutes time half of them stood in the tunnel   behind the wall containing the mayhem . One hundred and twenty seconds pass and the job was done.   They stood complete in their human form safely tucked away from those with   the intent to cause discord.

Inside the room they had exited Trychele and the "Quadrians"   came bursting through the door. Reducing the twelve inch thick wooden plank holding the grand oak doors shut to splinters. For those unfortunate enough to not have been struck down in battle trying to escape the fortress this was their death warrants.   The few body guards left formed a band around the defenseless and attacked with no hope of returning to their homes.   For no one returned from battle with "quadrrians."

Trycehele their feared leader and the last to have been created, had the head and eyes of an eagle, the upper strength of a bear concealed in the fragile structure of a human with hands the changed to paws when necessary, and the lower half had the speed and agility of a panther as the rest of them did. Trychele didn't possess the error of love like the others, he just calculated, reasoned ,   but didn't feel.

"You rip these measly humans from limb to limb. I will find the child."

Prince Robert was running as   fast as his four foot nine inch legs could take him.   His golden silk elf shoes with bells on the tips were slowing him down. He had borrowed his fathers shoes for this day it was his job to fill them for the ailing king. *What a stupid idea he thought to himself.*
"Sir it would be helpful if you would pick up the pace!" Both guards agreed.

When the roar of Trychele echoed through the damp dark narrow musty   tunnel only lit by his security's special abilities of fluorescent irises for night warfare. Curious about the direction they were traveling he inquired

"Where are we going?"

"To the river."

"There is no river down here."

"To the river sir!"

Trychele shared the same upgrade his guards had but with much brighter voltage.   Light came through the tunnel like the sun illuminating a night's sky.

"Trychele" he whispered to the other as not frighten their charge.   Robert's shoes came flying pass him as did his small stature. "Yal can die if you want too." he shouted over his shoulder.

"Wait we need to catch up." They responded. As Trychele rounded the corner; converting from two legs to four. His fingers cupped, the nails grew his back arched forcing him to stoop and his legs shorten and bent to resemble a panthers.

"Let's play cat and mouse boys." He roared out.

Chapter 3

The ninety two Nissan 's continued purring after the unintentional forceful kiss at forty miles per an hour in fact it sounded better now then it had for the last month.

Christian wanted to cry out is everyone okay, but he couldn't get his mouth to move or his eyes to open.   He couldn't believe that he had allowed this to happen to his nephew's.   *Where was my mind?   Why was it on her? Her problems aren't mine? Wh h h ere am. .   ?* His thoughts trailed off. He felt no pain.

Jeremey opened his eyes . His neck refused to obey the command to turn. His little body felt like the weight of the world was on his shoulders literally.   His eyeballs began to burn like Habernero was being rubbed in them.   They felt so dry so much pain and then there was nothing. No thought , no pain.

Neilson was sitting in the back seat on the opposite side of impact.   He was in excellent condition or so he thought.   He spoke

" Fish fly over the dam."   He said with the intent of saying   *is everyone okay.*   To him it sounded perfectly okay.   Since no one was conscious it didn't matter. There was no answer. Neilsons assumed his uncle and brother were being hard to get along with, therefore he focused his attention on trying to see his mother's house.   Like the other two occupants on the old Nissan he discovered his movement was limited to his mouth. His heart beating four times it natural rate he   reposed the question. " The trees suggest the path to safety."   He waited a few more seconds and tried again this time he yelled at the top of his lungs.   " And the river is the key."   Neilson wanted to draw in a breath to speak again, but nothing came in, he blacked out .

Christian heard Neilson's first question and giggled in his mind. *My mind.   Oh my goodness my mind.   It's awake.   I can think.* He was elated.

Neilson blacked out but . . .

Chapter 4

"Sir! We have found another way out."

The chubby snow blinding white man that walked with a stride of deadly charisma even at eighty nine, suggested to his murderous dictator leader.

"I don't want hear this non sense again."

"Sir!" he pleaded "This is no nonsense. You don't have to die you can save your family."

The white haired butterball took a step forward almost falling on his lab coat. A general stood between them with his service weapon drawn.

"I am not foolish or senile. And I do not wished to be patronized. "

"Shoot him." the dictator ordered.

"But I was there from the beginning.   I can help you."

"Believe me Scott I'm helping you."

A statuesque blond entered the bunker where her husband stood.   She was annoyed to have been dragged from the breakfast table without eating a morsel. To add to the pesky

request from her husband he required that she bring his brats with him.

"What do you want?" She spat out. "We are all here."

Three red dots appeared on each family member's head, so fast   not even the general knew what happen until the mist of grey matter and blood mist sprinkled his forehead. Still in shock the general turned his gun on the dictator.

"It was an honor sir."

"Shoot me! D . . ." The general hated a dirty mouth.

The scientist was more than confused , and the lab coat he took great care to keep as white as him was now a lovely shade between red and pink in the front. General towered over him by a foot and two inches and was now looking down at the part in his hair.   He used the classic comb over.   Cowering in fear for his own life he rehashed his suggestion   to the only one left in power. The general didn't talk for a whole sixty seconds. When he did choose his opening words there was   a sigh of relief on his part.

"He was crazy." he pointed to the corpse. "So are you American born scientist, but I'm desperate. You prove to me that your portal exist and   I will bring your pretty little young wife to you . She will go with us."

The two unlikely pair a batty scientist, and   a general who dealt only in realities, walked to a destination way more unique than them.

Chapter 5

A sole arm flopped about like a fish out of water. It's finger nails dug into the damp soil in an attempt to find the rest of it's body, then began patting the ground in search of a sign of the missing limbs. Thirty minutes later a leg popped up about fifteen inches from the arm and hand. Christian's head popped up clear of thought and awake, but where was his body.

"Where's my body?"

"I see Neilson's hand?"

"What happened to us? How are we alive? Are you okay Jeremy?!"

"Where's Neilson?"

"Neilson! Neilson!"

"Uncle where is my body ?!"

"I don't know Jeremy. Don't panic. I'm sure everything will be okay."

The trees rustled in the breeze.

"What was that uncle.   It's a bear that is going to eat us isn't it?"

"No."   He could feel nervous shivers send his body into convulsions. He hated to be helpless.   Especially with his nephews.   He needed to brandish a weapon for protection , be it a twig or a stone.   He couldn't just lay here.

In his peripheral he saw his leg come into arm's reach. He snatched it up and attached his body together like the ten piece puzzle he so enjoyed in first grade. Happy to be back on his feet or just to have feet he decided to take his extremities for a test run to find his missing relatives. He remembered seeing Neilson just three feet away from his landing.   If he could get this stupid leg to cooperate, just maybe he could get somewhere.

At first he thought the leg was not his, but when he looked down they looked to be wearing the yellow tennis shoes with lime green shoe strings that he normally wore when he was with the kids.   They loved those laces so much.   While he walked what seemed to be an eternity he reminisced over the times they had spent together. What was the fore most memory was them racing through the aisles over the well worn aisles in the value store.   They were determined to buy something nice for their uncle.   Something as silly as them Neilson had said. Each trip to the store with Uncle had a theme. The reasoning behind a long shopping trip with a theme started with Neilson's desire for a giant lollipop from the magic kingdom in Orlando Flordia. He wanted a lollipop and his mom wanted a bigger check to cover captian crunch andpeanut butter. That was the game today. Neilson heard his brother whining about a lollipop trip and asked if he could go on a gum shopping trip.   It was a silly day since their father had reopened a custody case and the days to follow would be anything but carefree. Once again they would be deciding between mom and dad, judge, law, and kindness. He wanted them to have this memory to hold onto during the interviews and descisions. He remembered they were   Mentioning holding on Christian glanced around at his surroundings.   Tree boughs were happily lazing about slouched over on each other as if his

speed were causing them to bend.   The sheer thought of it made his stomach bubble with laughter.

"Me speeding by them."   He struggled to pronounce between the escaping chuckles.

Although if he looked around him he didn't remember seeing any of these surroundings when his head literally fell in from the upper atmosphere. Clouds comparable to marshmallows, grasses that flowed like a river in the cooling breeze and felt like pillows of down feathers stuffed in cotton balls welcomed the indent of his bobble sized dome.

The hospitality of this world stopped there. An arrow whizzed by his head nearly lopping off an ear.

"What the . . .?"

"Hold there!"   echoed out.

Both his hands shot up in the air which was a surprise to him since he had not attached them and he did not land with them. At least that is how he remembered it, but then again he wasn't sure where he was so to go as far as assuming anything at this point would most certainly prove the old saying true about assumptions true. Minus the curious issues with his hands there was the more pressing issue of deadly arrows possibly being lodged in delicate anatomy.

" Where did that come from?"

To the right were trees and no discernible figure. "Nathaniel!" he called out for his nephew. "Nathaniel! Where are you?"

"Christian! Christian!" echoed.

Nathaniel plopped down in the meadow near the fours river. These areas were within the second sector of Flyaringaron. This area was the only one worth warring over. It was protected by a portion of each quadrants volunteer army. The three foreigners arrived on the day Trycel's tribe was patrolling their Eden.

Sitting on the banks of the river. Neilson buried his toes into the crystals sparkling sand, but he found the dirt to be tough. Particles scraped his big toe. Droplets of blood splattered on the points of the gleaming beach particles. Light shone on the sparkle crystalline shores.

"Pink diamonds." He half whispered fearful any noise would shatter the ballet of light performing before his eyes.

Puffy underdeveloped malformed cloud over shadowed the day luminary. The recital concluded with an extraordinary release of thermal energy they had received from the sunlight in waves of harmonious choral sound.

Standing beneath the canopy of the forest that the uncle and nephew were linking around. The nephew was on the west side of paradise while the adult was skirting the north east coner of the tree land.

"They are teenage Columbus clouds." The little boy said to Christian.

Christian's heart nearly jumped out of his chest at the sight of the little boy. He wasn't sure if he was hallucinating, if it was magic, or his brain chemistry.

"And you are?" No matter what this was there was no need to be impolite.

The boy smirked, and scoffed at his hand offered for a handshake. The withdrawn hand hung like the spontaneous heavy fog in the sky both warned of an ominous declaration.

Raindrops accumulate, thunder can be heard
Will the fog mean
The beginning of
THE END